For my sister Kathleen Clark   MM

For Mum and Dad   DM

VIKING

Published by the Penguin Group

Viking Penguin, a division of Penguin Books USA Inc.,

375 Hudson Street, New York, New York 10014, U.S.A.

Penguin Books Australia Ltd, Ringwood, Victoria, Australia

Penguin Books Canada Ltd, 2801 John Street, Markham, Ontario, Canada L3R 1B4

Penguin Books (N.Z.) Ltd, 182–190 Wairau Road, Auckland 10, New Zealand

This edition first published in Great Britain by ABC, 1991

First American edition published in 1991

1   3   5   7   9   10   8   6   4   2

Text copyright © Maryann Macdonald, 1991

Illustrations copyright © David McTaggart, 1991

All rights reserved

ISBN 0-670-83920-5

Printed in Hong Kong by Imago Services (H.K.) Ltd.

Ben at the Beach

Written by Maryann Macdonald
Illustrated by David McTaggart

VIKING

Grandma was taking Ben and Charlotte to the beach.

Ben had a new fishing rod. "I am going to catch a big, big fish!" he said.

Charlotte had a bucket and a shovel. "Me dig," she said. "Dig big."

At last they got to the beach.

"May I go fishing now, Grandma?" Ben asked.

"All right, Ben," said Grandma.

So Ben took his fishing rod and went off to the dock.

"Sorry," a man on the dock said. "No children allowed."

Ben walked back to the beach.

He tried to cast his line into the deep water where big fish live. But his line was too short.

He tried to catch little fish in the shallow water. But the little fish would not bite.

"Ben," called Grandma. "Come and play with Charlotte now!"

"Oh, well," said Ben. And he went to take Charlotte wading in the cool water.

But Charlotte did not like the water.
She would not go in. "Monsters!" she
yelled and held on to Ben.

"Nice water," said Ben. He splashed gently.
"BAD WATER!" yelled Charlotte. She started to cry.

"Don't cry," said Ben. He got Charlotte's bucket
and shovel. "Dig?" he asked. "Dig big?"
"Yes," said Charlotte.
So Ben dug a big hole with Charlotte.

They made a wall and put seashells and stones on it.
Last of all, Ben dug a moat.
"Now," he said to Charlotte, "comes the *best part*!"

He took the bucket and waded
into the shallow water.

He filled it with water and
poured the water into the moat.

Charlotte saw little fish shining in the
sunlight. "Pretty!" she said. "More!"
"Your turn," said Ben.

He took Charlotte's hand. Charlotte held
Ben's hand tightly. She waded with him
slowly into the water.

She took the bucket and filled it with water.

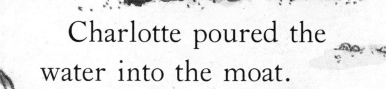

Charlotte poured the
water into the moat.

Then she smiled proudly at Ben.

"Congratulations!" said a man. "You win first prize in the sand castle contest."

The first prize was a boat! Grandma
helped them blow it up. Then they
all got in. Grandma paddled.

Charlotte watched out for sea monsters.

And Ben caught a big fish in the deep water.

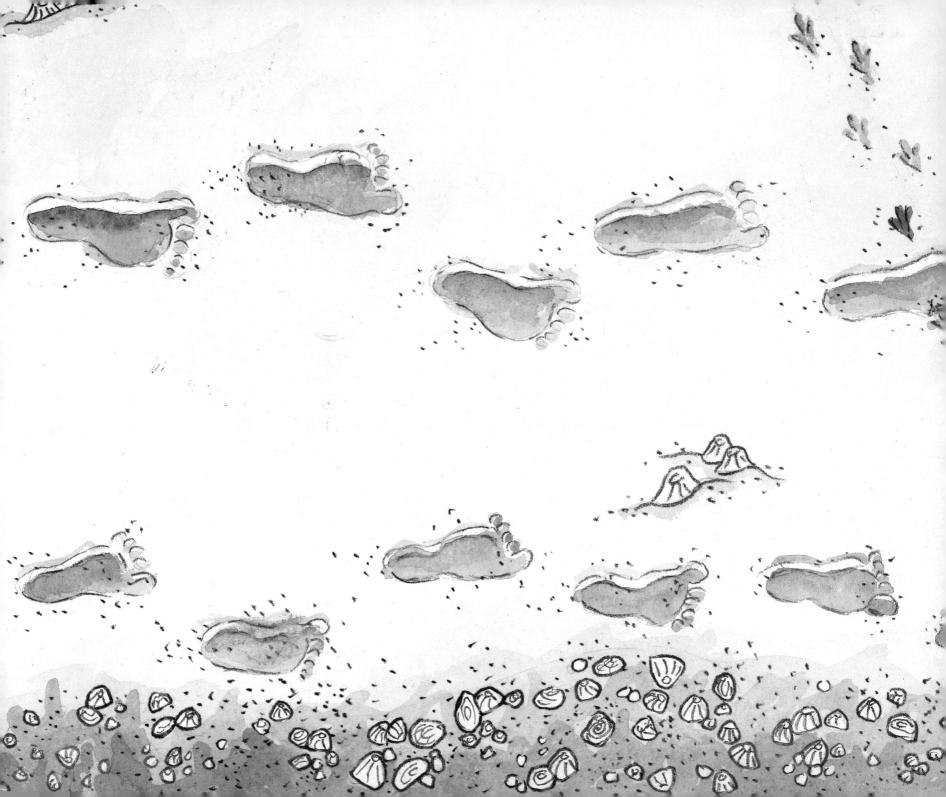